←YOU CHOOSE→

# BATMAN™

DC
COMICS™
SUPER
HEROES

STONE ARCH BOOKS
a capstone imprint

You Choose Stories: Batman
is published by Stone Arch Books,
A Capstone Imprint
1710 Roe Crest Drive
North Mankato, Minnesota 56003
www.capstonepub.com

Cataloging-in-Publication Data is available
on the Library of Congress website.
ISBN: 978-1-4342-9706-8 (library binding)
ISBN: 978-1-4342-9710-5 (paperback)
ISBN: 978-1-4965-0210-0 (eBook)

Summary: At a Gotham City charity event, the Riddler
kidnaps several wealthy guests and demands a huge
ransom. With your help, Batman will solve the puzzle
of The Riddler's Ransom!

Printed in the United States of America in North Mankato, Minnesota.
040115      008873R

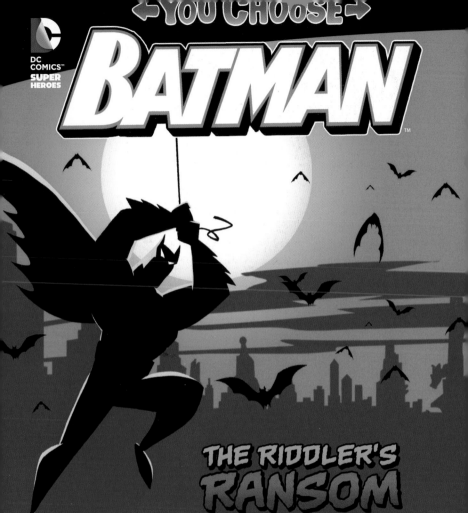

# YOU CHOOSE

## DC COMICS SUPER HEROES

# BATMAN™

## THE RIDDLER'S RANSOM

Batman created by Bob Kane

written by
**Blake Hoena**

illustrated by
**Ethen Beavers**

# ←YOU CHOOSE→

# BATMAN™

At a Gotham City charity event, the Riddler kidnaps several wealthy guests and demands money for their return. Only YOU can help the Dark Knight solve the puzzle of *The Riddler's Ransom*!

Follow the directions at the bottom of each page. The choices YOU make will change the outcome of the story. After you finish one path, go back and read the others for more Batman adventures!

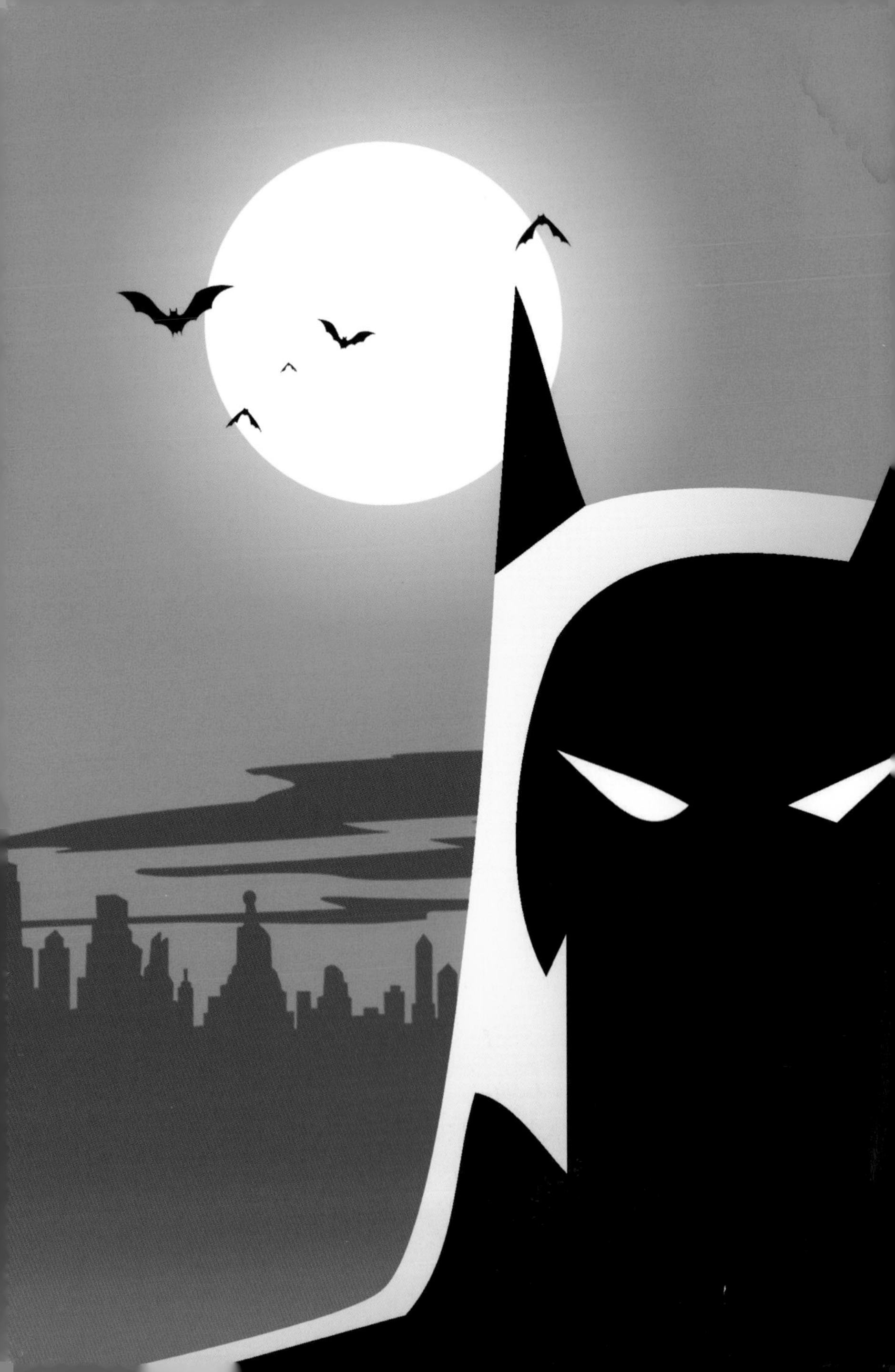

High up in Wayne Tower, some of the richest people in the world have gathered. Princes and princesses mingle with Wall Street investors. South American business owners brag to European philanthropists. Engineers from North America and Asia discuss new technologies.

Bored by it all, billionaire Bruce Wayne stands off to one side and looks out the ballroom's ceiling-high windows. Neon lights flicker below, lighting up Gotham City. But one light is absent from the night sky: the Bat-Signal atop police headquarters.

Turn the page.

Bruce half wishes that the signal would blink on. The Bat-Signal would give him a reason to excuse himself from this stuffy affair, because secretly he is Batman, the Dark Knight. He helps keep the streets of Gotham City safe.

On nights like this, he'd rather be down in the city's crime-infested alleyways than hobnobbing with the world's elite. The wrongdoings of criminals are much easier to deal with than the whims of the rich and famous.

"Master Wayne," Alfred says, interrupting his thoughts. "It's time for everyone to be seated."

Bruce turns to his loyal butler. "Very well, Alfred," he replies.

"Have you prepared your speech for tonight, sir?" the butler asks.

The blank look on Bruce's face is answer enough. Alfred reaches into his suit jacket pocket and pulls out a set of neat note cards.

"Perhaps you can use these," he says, handing over the notes.

"Thank you," Bruce replies.

Bruce isn't sure why he's on edge tonight. After all, this event was his idea — a charity ball to support the Martha Wayne Foundation. Named in honor of his mother, the organization helps feed and educate children in Gotham City.

Bruce had invited his wealthy guests here tonight to support him in expanding the foundation's goals throughout the world. Maybe he is just stressed because of how important the foundation's success is to him.

Or maybe there is something else.

Bruce glances quickly around the ballroom. People are taking their places at the tables.

The caterers are clustered in small groups along the outer walls of the room. He is somewhat annoyed that they aren't filling his guests' glasses. But then again, he doesn't want the clinking of glasses drowning out his speech.

Bruce heads toward a small podium near the center of the hall.

Turn the page.

A large video screen has been set up on the stage. He will use it to show how much his guests contribute at this charity event.

All eyes are on him as his long strides carry him across the room. As Bruce nears the podium, he shuffles his note cards and clears his throat. He is ready to kick off this event with a bang.

Then suddenly . . .

## *KA-BOOM!*

Before Bruce can reach the platform, an explosion rips open the ceiling directly above the stage. Bruce staggers backward. Debris rains down from the ceiling, nearly striking the billionaire. Bruce shields his eyes with his arms. All around him, he hears people coughing and screaming, but he cannot see them through the thick dust.

When the dust finally clears, a man stands onstage, wearing a green suit and wielding a question-mark cane.

It's the Riddler!

Turn to page 12.

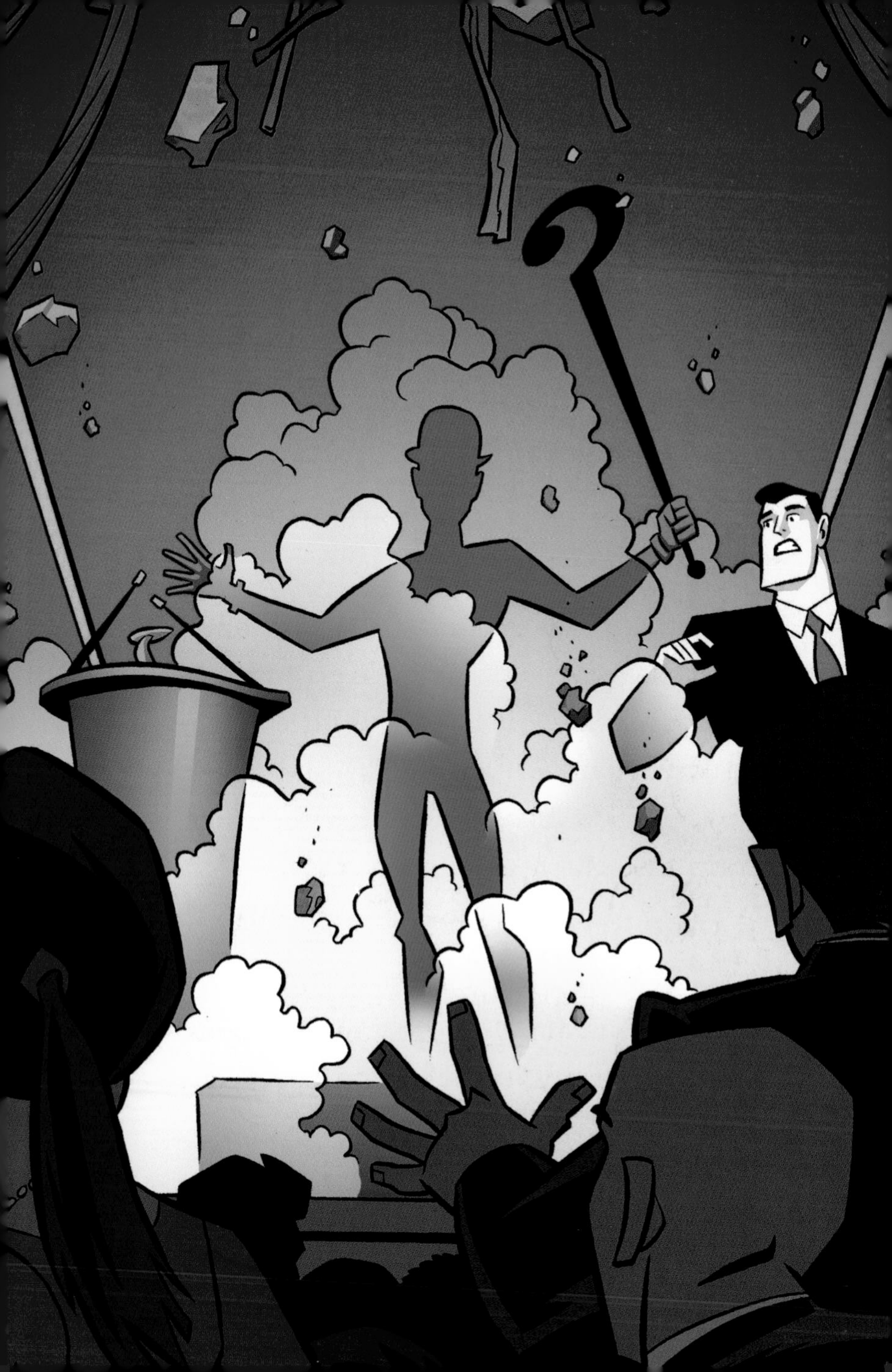

The world's most clever criminal moves back and forth across the stage, surveying the crowd with a wicked grin. Then the Riddler strides toward the podium and grasps the microphone in his hands.

"Testing, testing. Is this thing on?" the villain says, tapping the microphone.

Feedback squeals through the ballroom's speakers, causing the guests to cover their ears.

"Good, I have your attention," the Riddler begins. "So now, who do we have here tonight?" The villain peers out at the guests once again. "The world's rich and famous. Glad I dressed for the occasion." He tugs on his black tie, which has a green question mark on it.

Meanwhile, Bruce backs away from the center of the room and blends into the crowd. He wants to avoid drawing attention to himself and see what the Riddler will do before he acts.

As he does, Bruce notices that the caterers shed their black tuxedo shirts and white bow ties.

Underneath, they wear purple T-shirts with large, black question marks on their chests.

*They're the Riddler's henchmen,* thinks Bruce.

The henchmen leave the spots where they had clustered against the walls and weave through the tables to patrol the room. Whenever anyone tries to get up, they are promptly shoved back into their seats. Some people try to run for the exits, but the henchmen have already sealed them off.

Bruce slowly makes his way to the back of the room. He's trying to decide his next move.

Suddenly, Bruce bumps into Alfred along the far wall, near the kitchen doors.

"Where did you find these caterers?" the billionaire asks his loyal butler.

"Online," Alfred replies. "They had exceptional reviews. They were called Red Smith Deli."

"Hmm," Bruce thinks aloud for a moment. "An anagram for Riddle Me This."

Turn the page.

"Well, I —" Alfred stammers. "You requested fusion dishes from around the world, and their kimchi pasta is to die for."

"Let's hope you're wrong about that last part," Bruce says.

If Bruce stays to learn what the Riddler is planning, turn to page 15.

If Bruce sneaks away to change into Batman, turn to page 35.

Knowing the Riddler, Bruce doesn't want to sneak away. Not just yet. He knows that this is all part of a more elaborate scheme. The best way to find out what the Riddler is up to is to stay close to the action.

"You're probably all wondering why I am gracing you with my presence," the Riddler says, slowly strutting across the stage and spinning his cane. "Well, it's quite simple."

The super-villain motions to the big screen on the podium. It glows with a series of blinking lights. The screen shows five red bars with green dollar signs next to them.

"Seeing that you are some of the world's most powerful and wealthiest people and are all ready to empty your pockets in the name of charity," he explains, "I figured you could donate to my favorite cause . . . me!"

The Riddler removes his green bowler hat and holds it up in the air.

"Now all I need is a volunteer. Anyone . . . ?"

**Turn the page.**

The partygoers are silent. Most crouch lower into their seats, trying not to be noticed by the madman on stage.

"Nobody?" says the Riddler. "Well, then I guess the choice is mine."

With his cane, the Riddler motions to his henchmen. The crooks begin circling the audience. Before long they grab a tall man by the collar of his suit.

"Too tall," shouts the Riddler from the stage.

Another henchman points toward a short woman seated at a nearby table.

"Too short," says the Riddler.

Suddenly, two henchmen grab Bruce by the arms. Bruce struggles for a moment. He knows he could easily overpower the men, but then people might discover his secret identity as the Dark Knight.

"Ah," the Riddler finally says, "just right."

The henchmen drag Bruce to the front of the stage at their boss's request.

"Our host, Bruce Wayne, will do me the honor," the Riddler says with a bow. "I'm going to have you draw names out of my hat. Those lucky enough to be selected will join me for a night on the town."

The villain laughs and lowers his hat toward Bruce. Then he jerks it away just as Bruce is about to reach in to draw a name. Bruce is puzzled by the villain's plan.

"There is a catch, however," the Riddler says. "Those who remain will need to pledge one million dollars every half hour, which I will keep track of on this monitor." He points to the upper right-hand corner of the screen, which shows a timer. "Every time that goal is met, I will release one of my guests. If not . . . well . . . let's not talk about that just yet."

The Riddler lowers his hat to Bruce, but again pulls it back as Bruce is about to reach in.

"Oh, and if anyone attempts to leave before my game is done," the Riddler says, "there will be *explosive* consequences."

**Turn the page.**

The Riddler lowers his hat again. Bruce just looks at him this time.

"I won't pull it away again — promise," the Riddler says.

Bruce draws out a piece of paper and reads off, "Tai Nakamura."

*A leading video game developer,* Bruce thinks, remembering one of his wealthier guests.

Two of the Riddler's henchmen pull a tall, thin man from his seat and lead him out of the ballroom. Then Tai's picture suddenly appears on top of one of the colored bars on the monitor.

Bruce draws three more names, and three more guests are led away, with their names appearing on the Riddler's monitor.

"Please," says Bruce, "these people don't need to be involved. Take me instead, Riddler. I have all the money you could possibly want."

"And I just decided that since you've been so helpful, as a reward, my fifth and final guest will be you, Mr. Wayne," the Riddler announces.

Two henchmen grab Bruce by the arms and lead him away. He is taken out of the ballroom and dragged into an elevator that drops down toward the lobby of Wayne Tower.

If Bruce attempts to escape now, turn to page 20.

If Bruce continues along with the Riddler's plan, turn to page 22.

Bruce has little time as the elevator races downward to the lobby, but now is the moment to act. He must escape to foil the Riddler's plans before it's too late.

The henchmen on either side of him stare straight ahead. In a split second, Bruce elbows one in the gut and kicks the legs out from the other. A second later, both of the men are unconscious from the fight.

The Dark Knight then opens the escape hatch on the top of the elevator. Using his martial arts skills, Bruce leaps up, grabs the ledge of the opening, and then pulls himself out of the top of the elevator.

When the elevator opens in the lobby below, the henchmen there are surprised to see two of their own, groaning on the floor.

*\*\**

After climbing through the nearest emergency hatch, Bruce quickly heads to his office in the upper floors of Wayne Tower.

On a shelf in the corner of the room is a bust of William Shakespeare. Bruce tilts it backward to reveal a red switch. He flicks it on.

### *FWIP!*

A secret door slides open behind his desk, revealing an emergency Batsuit.

Turn to page 37.

When the elevator doors open, the henchmen quickly lead Bruce to a green stretch limo that is parked out front. He is shoved inside, and the door is slammed shut behind him.

Bruce sits quiet and still, trying to take in all that is happening.

Suddenly, the locks on the doors click. Shortly afterward, the front doors open, but he can't see who is getting in — the glass divider is closed. Rather, Bruce feels the car shift under the weight of two people jostling their way in.

Then the car lurches forward.

The windows are tinted black, so Bruce can't see out. But the secret super hero keeps track of the car's twists and turns.

At one point, the limo slowly rises upward and then slopes back down.

*We're going over a bridge,* Bruce thinks. *Maybe the Sprang Bridge.*

There's also the faint smell of sea salt in the air, and he hears the blast of a tugboat.

When the door finally opens, Bruce is greeted by a stun gun.

"Out," he is ordered.

Bruce must quickly decide whether to escape or continue playing along with his captors.

If Bruce tries to escape, turn to page 24.

If Bruce continues to play along with his captors, turn to page 27.

Bruce has had enough of playing along. It's time for action. It's time for him to become Batman and thwart the Riddler's plans.

As he gets out of the car, Bruce pretends to stumble forward. The henchman reaches out to steady him. Then Bruce delivers a blow to the henchman's jaw, sending the man reeling backwards. *POW!*

Turn to page 26.

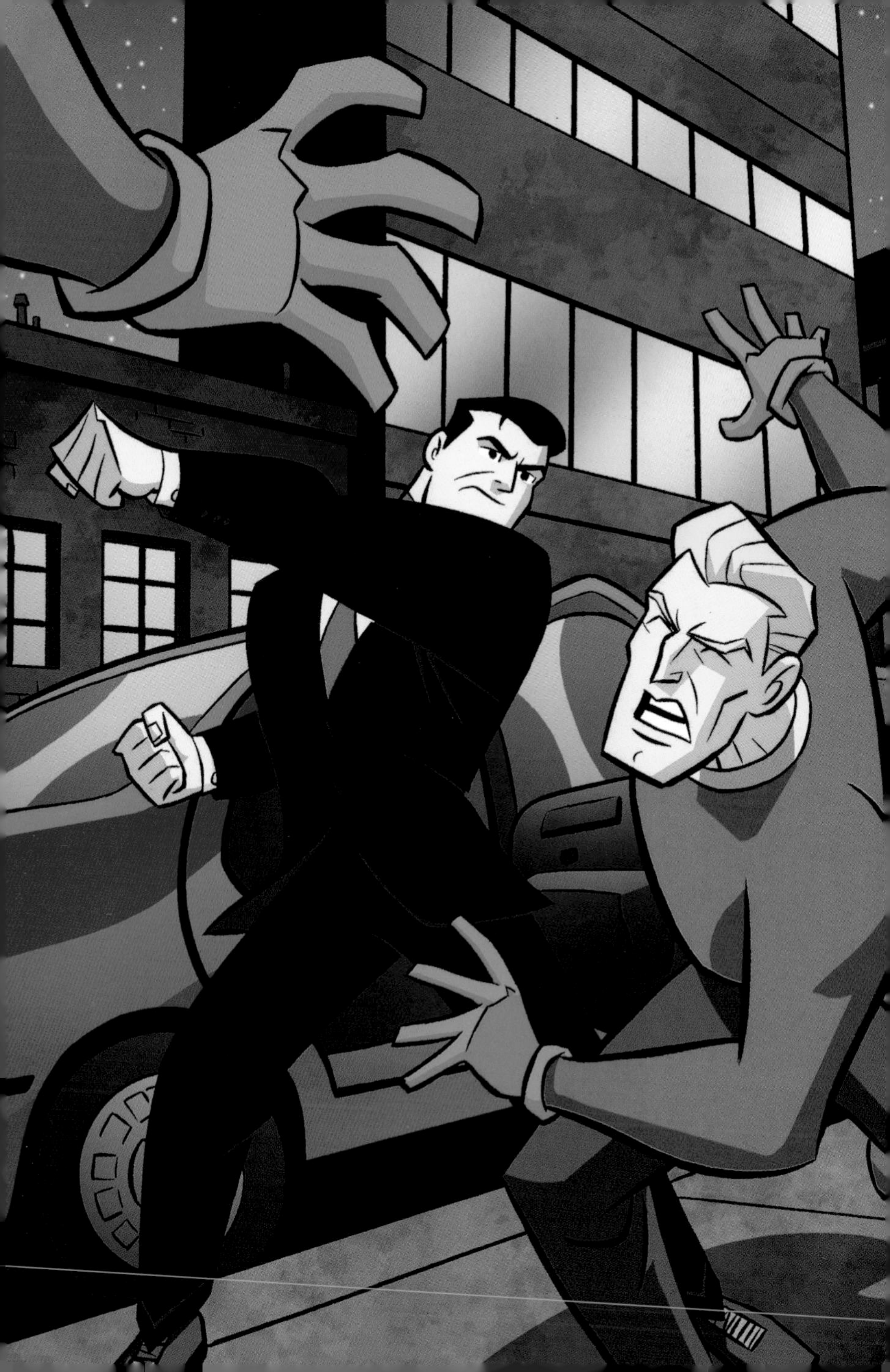

Bruce is about to go for the knockout blow when the stun gun strikes him in the ribs.

### *ZAP! ZAP! ZAP!*

Bruce forgot about the second henchman, who stands off to his right. He holds a smoking stun gun.

Bruce collapses to the ground, writhing in pain. He'll never recover in time to stop the Riddler now.

"You weren't supposed to zap him," the one henchman says while rubbing his jaw.

"That's better than what the Riddler had planned for him."

**THE END**

To follow another path, turn to page 7.

Bruce steps out of the car. As he does, he sees the second henchman to his right with a stun gun lowered at him. He stands far enough away that there is no way Bruce could take down both of the henchmen before one zaps him. The secret super hero continues to play along.

Glancing around, Bruce notices that he's at Roger's Yacht Basin. He is led onto one of the yachts, *The Orchid*. Then he's shoved below deck.

"Sit!" a man orders.

The only piece of furniture in the cabin is a small wooden chair. Bruce takes a seat. While one henchman keeps a stun gun leveled at him, the other wraps a rope around his chest and arms and ties his hands behind his back.

Off to the side, Bruce sees a blank monitor with a keyboard and black case attached to it.

Before the henchmen leave, one drops a folded note into Bruce's lap.

"Activate the bomb," the other speaks into a phone. On the monitor, white lights flash 0:10.

Turn the page.

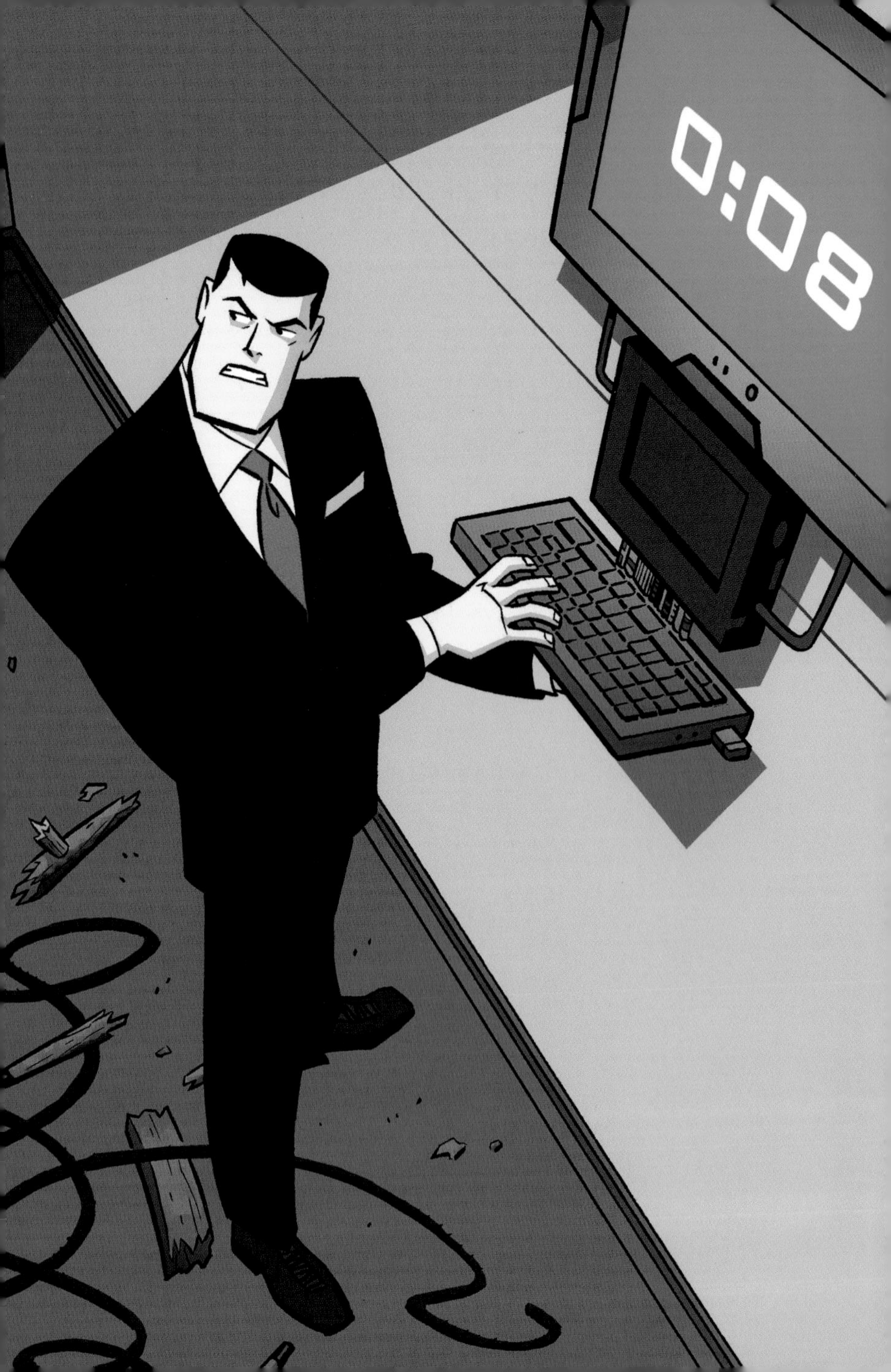
0:08

As soon as he is alone, Bruce goes into action. He leans forward in the chair so that all of its legs are off the ground. Then he leaps up as best he can. When he lands, he lets the wooden chair take the brunt of his weight. It shatters beneath him. He quickly disentangles himself from the ropes and broken pieces of chair.

Once free of his constraints, Bruce reads the note: WHAT RUNS BUT NEVER GETS TIRED?

*A riddle,* he thinks. *Meant for Batman.* Then Bruce turns to the monitor, with the black case and keyboard.

*This must be some sort of bomb,* he thinks.

Before he reaches the monitor, the numbers on the display start winding down.

"A motion sensor must have set it off," he curses under his breath.

There is a keyboard, so he guesses he needs to type in an answer to the note's riddle. The seconds tick down. 0:05 . . . 0:04 . . .

If Bruce types "NOSE," turn to page 34.
If Bruce types "WATER," turn to page 30.

0:03 . . .

Bruce types *WATER* on the keyboard. Each letter lights up on the screen just below the countdown.

0:02 . . .

Then he hits Enter.

Suddenly, the countdown stops.

Nothing.

His guess is right. *Water, like that from a tap, runs but never tires,* Bruce thinks.

While he is not in his Batman uniform yet, Bruce still has small communication device hidden in his wristwatch.

"Alfred?" he whispers into it.

A few second pass. Then he hears a muffled voice.

"Here, sir," the butler replies.

"What's happening there?" Bruce asks.

"It's utter chaos, sir," Alfred replies. "Shortly after you were taken away, the Riddler left. Then everyone started arguing about whether to pay for the release of his hostages."

"I'll need the Batmobile to come pick me up," Bruce says.

"I've already activated it remotely," says Alfred. "It's locked onto your signal and heading your way."

Turn to page 33.

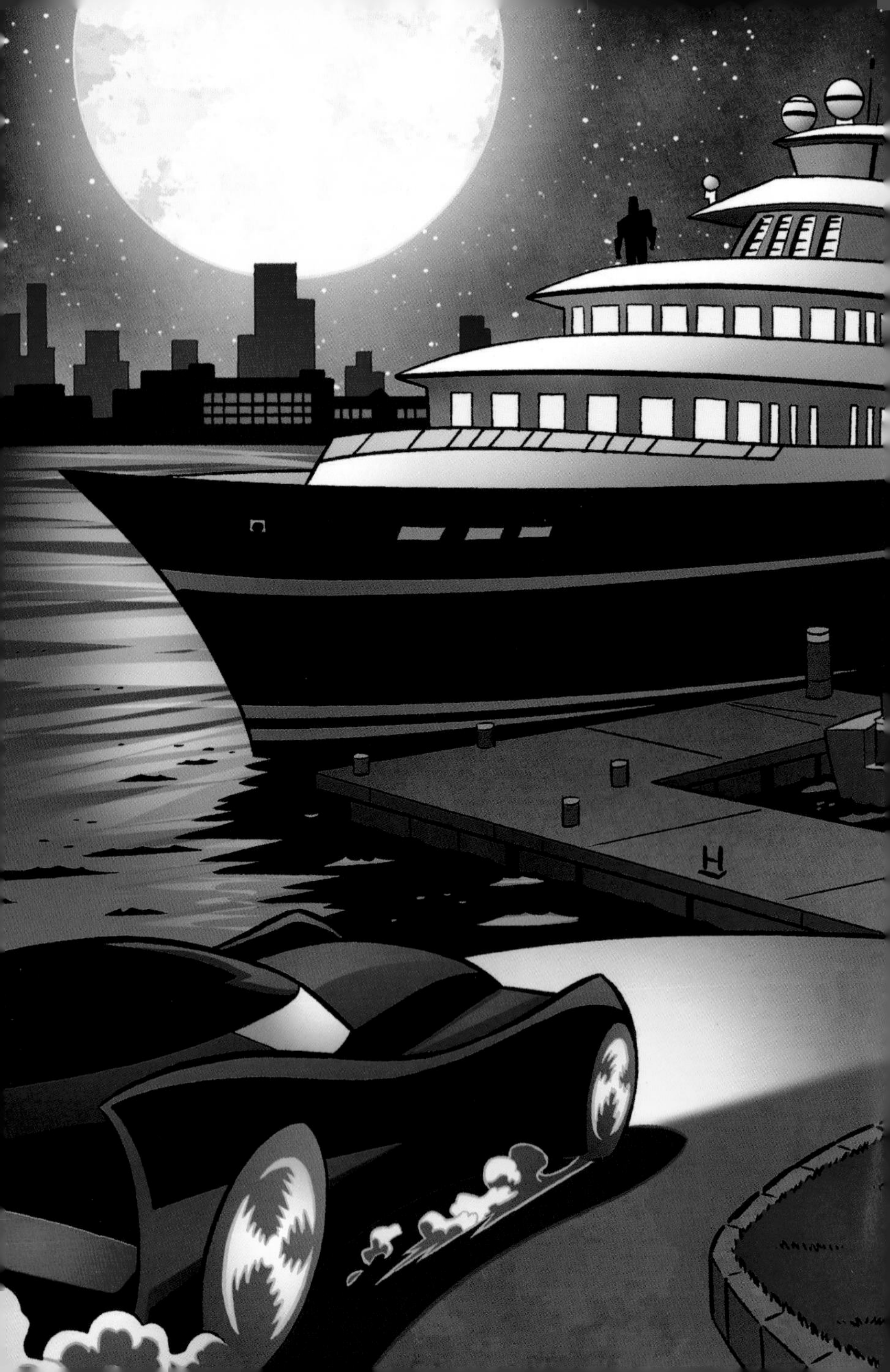

Bruce darts up the stairs and onto the yacht's deck. Quickly approaching in the distance, he sees a pair of familiar headlights.

Then Bruce hears the roar of a high-powered engine coming toward the docks.

### VROOOM! VROOOM!

It's the Batmobile!

It's time for his alter ego to come out and play with the Riddler.

Turn to page 44.

0:03 . . .

Bruce types *NOSE* on the keyboard, thinking of a runny nose. Each letter lights up on the screen just below the countdown.

0:02 . . .

Then he hits Enter.

0:00 . . .

Suddenly, the numbers switch to all zeroes. They flash.

*Wrong answer,* is the last thought that enters Bruce's mind.

Bruce barely has time to escape the ship as the bomb explodes. A ball of flame lights up the night as the yacht explodes. Until this mess is cleaned up, the Riddler will remain on the loose.

**THE END**

To follow another path, turn to page 7.

While everyone's attention is on the Riddler, Bruce quickly ducks through one of the service doors and into the kitchen. It is empty, as all the caterers are now out in the ballroom.

Then Bruce heads to his office in the upper levels of Wayne Tower. On a shelf in the corner of the room is a bust of William Shakespeare. He tilts it backward. A red switch is hidden underneath.

**BEEP!** Bruce flips the switch, and a secret door slides open behind his desk, revealing an emergency Batsuit.

As the Dark Knight, the super hero is ready to confront the Riddler.

"Alfred, are you there?" Batman speaks through the headset in his cowl.

Seconds pass, then he hears a muffled voice on the other end.

"I'm here, sir."

"How are the guests?" Batman asks. "Is everyone all right?"

Turn the page.

"They're panicked, sir," Alfred replies. "Shortly after you left, the Riddler took away five of them as hostages. He's asking a million dollars ransom every half hour for their release."

"Is he still there?" asks Bruce.

"No, he departed moments ago."

Turn to page 39.

As Batman, he now feels ready to deal with the Riddler.

"Alfred, are you there?" Batman speaks through the headset in his cowl.

Seconds pass, then he hears a muffled voice.

"Here, sir."

"Has my escape been noticed?" Batman asks.

"Yes, a couple of the Riddler's henchmen rushed in shortly after you were taken away," Alfred replies.

"Is he still there?"

"No, he departed moments ago, taking a fifth hostage."

Turn to page 39.

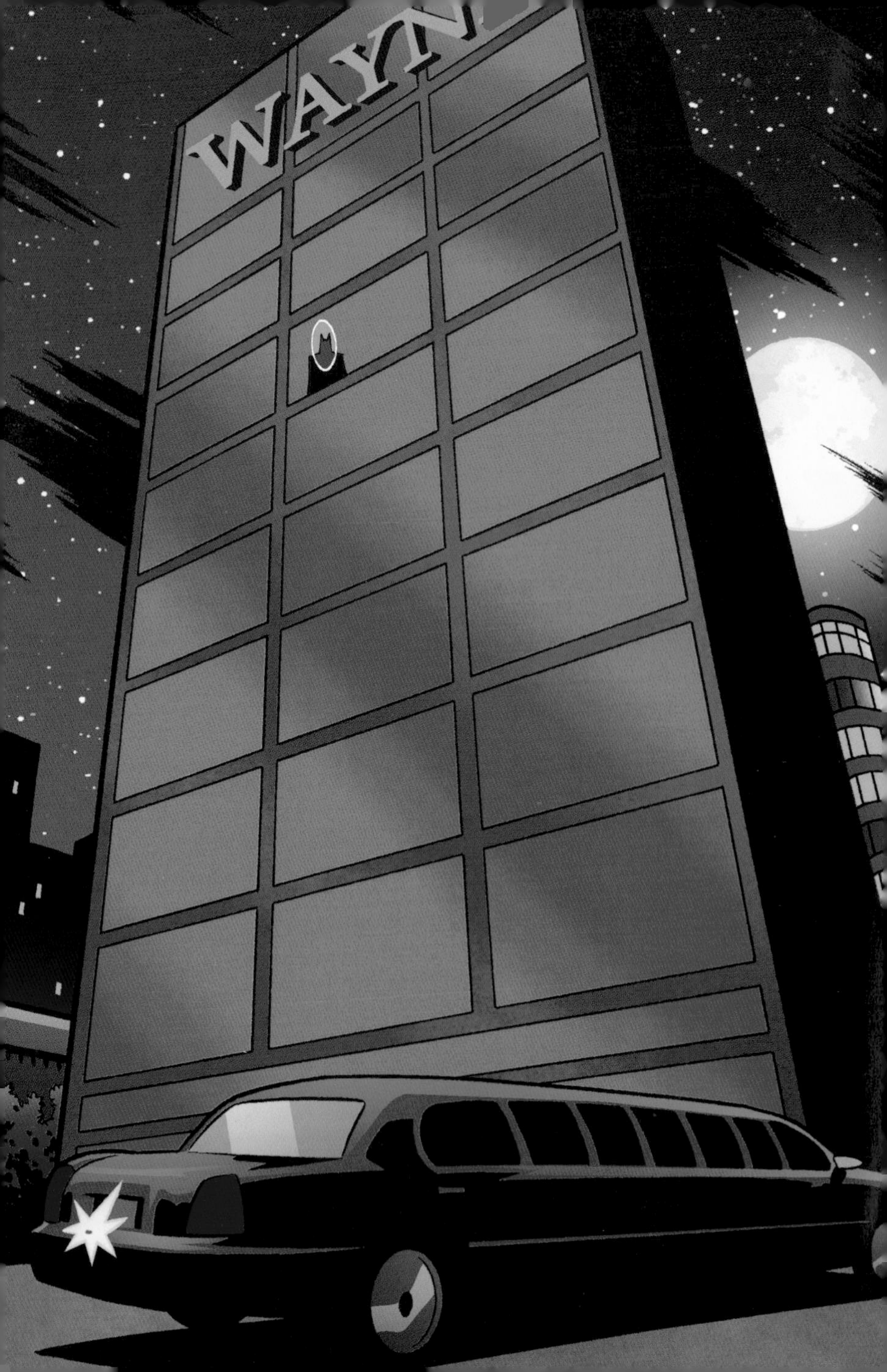
WAYN

As he and Alfred talk, Batman is in motion. He finds a window overlooking the front entrance. A green stretch limousine is parked below on the street.

*That has to be the Riddler's,* he thinks.

The Dark Knight pulls a small laser from his Utility Belt and cuts a circle in the window. Then, taking a high-tech tracking device from his Utility Belt, he shoots it through the hole at the limousine below.

"I'll need the Batmobile," Bruce says into his headset.

"I've already activated it remotely, sir. It's on its way," Alfred assures him.

\*\*\*

Moments later, the Dark Knight reaches the main floor of Wayne Tower as the Batmobile pulls up. A door slides open, and the super hero leaps into the driver's seat. He flips a switch on the high-tech vehicle's control panel, and a screen lights up in front of him.

Turn the page.

The monitor on the control panel shows a high-tech, detailed map Gotham City. On that map a green light flashes — the tracking device on the Riddler's limousine.

The limousine heads north over the Sprang Bridge and makes its way to Roger's Yacht Basin.

### VROOOOOOM!

The Dark Knight slams his foot on the Batmobile's gas pedal. The vehicle's monstrous engine rumbles like thunder through the night. The tires spin and squeal as Batman speeds off into the darkness.

As he approaches Roger's Yacht Basin, the Dark Knight turns off the Batmobile's headlights. He lets his car roll to a stop in the shadows near the green limousine.

There is no one in sight.

The super hero goes to investigate. The limousine is empty.

Then the creak of a boat's hull rubbing against a pier draws his attention to the docks.

Batman turns to see two of the Riddler's henchmen stepping up onto the deck of one of the yachts, *The Orchid*. The super hero ducks into the shadows as the two men head his way.

Once they walk by his hiding spot, the Dark Knight leaps out. He lets out a whistle to get their attention.

"Huh?!" exclaim the two men, spinning around with their weapons drawn.

Unfortunately for them, the Dark Knight already has his weapon at the ready. With the flick of his wrist, Batman releases a Batarang.

### FWIP! FWIP!

The razor-sharp weapon zips through the air. Before the thugs can react, the Batarang strikes its target. It hits one thug's gun, and then ricochets and hits the other's. The henchmen's weapons fall to the ground.

With his enemies unarmed, the Dark Knight moves in for some hand-to-hand combat. No one can match his martial arts skills.

Turn the page.

### THWAP!

A kick to the stomach sends one of the henchmen reeling. The other tries reaching for a stun gun tucked into his belt, but Batman is on him before he can draw.

### SMACK!

Batman delivers a blow to the man's jaw, and he crumples on the ground.

Batman grabs hold of the other henchman.

"Is the Riddler in there?" he asks, looking over at *The Orchid*.

The henchman shakes his head no.

"Then who?" growls the Dark Knight.

"I dunno. One of the hostages."

That's all Batman needs to know. He takes a pair of handcuffs from his Utility Belt and binds the man. Then he rushes over to the yacht.

The super hero leaps on board and ducks down below deck. In the middle of the cabin sits a man tied to a chair.

To his right, Batman sees a monitor with red LED lights that read 0:10. There is a keyboard and a black case attached to the monitor.

*A bomb,* he thinks.

If Batman tries to disable the bomb first, turn to page 46.
If Batman helps the hostage first, turn to page 45.

Now, as Batman, he is ready to take on the Riddler.

The first guest the Riddler took away was Tai Nakamura, one of the world's richest and most successful video game developers.

*Only where did the Riddler take him?* Batman wonders.

The super hero flicks a switch, and a map of Gotham City appears on a screen in the Batmobile. He narrows in on the northern part of the city. Knowing how the Riddler likes to play games, leaving a trail of clues for him to follow, there are two locations he thinks that Tai might be located.

If Batman heads to the arcade at Amusement Mile, turn to page 51.

If Batman heads to the orchid display at Giordana Botanical Gardens, turn to page 55.

Batman strides over to the man. The super hero quickly checks to make sure there aren't any traps. All he sees is a note on the man's lap:

WHAT RUNS BUT NEVER GETS TIRED?

Batman glances over at the bomb. *This must be a clue to defuse it.*

He quickly unties the man.

"Go!" he says as he steps over to the bomb.

Suddenly, the numbers on the monitor start ticking down.

0:09 . . . 0:08 . . . 0:07 . . .

"A motion sensor must have set it off," he curses to himself.

There is a keyboard, so he guesses he needs to type in an answer to the note's riddle.

If Bruce types "WATER," turn to page 48.
If Bruce types "NOSE," turn to page 50.

Batman steps toward the bomb. Suddenly, the numbers start ticking down.

0:09 . . . 0:08 . . . 0:07 . . .

"A motion sensor must have set it off," he curses.

0:06 . . .

He glances back at the tied up man. No time to get him off the boat.

0:05 . . .

He glances back to the bomb. No time to defuse it.

0:04 . . .

Batman rips the monitor, the case, and the keyboard from the wall.

0:03 . . .

The super hero darts up to the deck.

0:02 . . .

He cocks his arm back and throws it all overboard.

0:01 . . .

*KA-BOOM!*

A geyser of water explodes in the harbor. Batman is safe, but he'll need time to clean up this mess. For now, the Riddler is free.

**THE END**

To follow another path, turn to page 7.

Batman types *WATER* on the keyboard. Each letter lights up on the screen just below the countdown. Then he hits Enter.

Suddenly, the countdown stops.

His guess is right. Water, like that from a tap, runs but never tires.

Batman darts up the stairs and onto the yacht's deck. The hostage is safely on land.

"Alfred, I rescued the last hostage that was taken," Batman says into his headset. "But there is no sign of the Riddler."

"What about the other hostages?" Alfred asked. "Your guests are arguing over who should pay the ransom. Not a cent has been raised for their release."

"Then we have less than half an hour to save Tai Nakamura. He was the first hostage taken."

"The game developer?" Alfred asks. "Did the Riddler leave any clues as to where he might be?"

As they talk, the Dark Knight dashes toward the Batmobile.

Batman leaps into the high-tech vehicle and then glances at the map of Gotham City still on the screen. He narrows it in on the northern part of the city.

"I have a couple ideas where to find him," Batman says.

If Batman heads to the arcade at Amusement Mile, turn to page 51.

If Batman heads to the orchid display at Giordana Botanical Gardens, turn to page 55.

0:03 . . .

Batman types *NOSE* on the keyboard. Each letter lights up on the screen just below the countdown.

0:02 . . .

Then he hits Enter.

0:00 . . .

Suddenly, the numbers switch to all zeroes. They flash.

*Wrong answer,* is the last thought that enters his mind. The bomb explodes. Shrapnel rips the yacht apart as the area is lit up with a ball of flame.

Batman barely makes it off alive. He floats in the harbor among the debris, wondering how he'll ever catch the Riddler now.

**THE END**

To follow another path, turn to page 7.

### *FWOOOOOOSH!*

The Dark Knight speeds off to the Amusement Mile. It is the location of the city's largest arcade and home to many of the games that Tai Nakamura developed. It seems like a logical choice to start.

The Dark Knight turns off the lights and lets the Batmobile coast to a stop once near the arcade. Jumping out, he quickly ducks into the shadows. Then Batman quickly finds his way to the back door.

It's closed.

The door is locked.

The super hero pulls out a lock pick from his Utility Belt and quickly jimmies the door open. Inside, the place is empty, yet the games are still lit up.

Sirens blare.

Bombs explode.

Engines rumble. The sounds are deafening.

Turn the page.

Batman slowly works his way through the arcade, looking for signs that either Tai or the Riddler are there.

Nothing.

*I must have gone to the wrong location,* the super hero thinks.

He should have gone to the Giordano Botanical Gardens. The name of the boat, *The Orchid*, back at Roger's Yacht Basin was his clue. The Riddler would not have put a hostage on that exact boat if it wasn't meant as a hint.

\*\*\*

Back in the Batmobile, Batman speeds away to the Giordano Botanical Gardens. On the drive, he looks up the garden's map on the Batmobile's computer. Then he asks for the "Orchid Display," to find the exact location.

As he pulls up, an explosion rips through one of the greenhouses, shattering glass and sending up a huge ball of flame.

*Too late,* Batman curses. *I failed.*

Just then, the Dark Knight spots a man moving among the ashes. It's Mr. Nakamura! He is safe.

Batman runs to his side, knowing next time he might not be so lucky.

If Batman continues to try to save the remaining hostages, turn to 54.

If the guests at Bruce Wayne's Charity Ball raise the ransom money, turn to page 59.

One hostage narrowly survived, and there are others that need saving. It is not time to give up. Not when people are still in danger. Not when the Riddler is still on the loose.

*He will pay for this,* Batman thinks.

"Alfred, who was the second hostage taken?" he asks.

"Steven Knight, owner of the Gotham Knights baseball team," his butler replies.

*Hmm,* Batman thinks and looks at the map of Gotham City.

"The Knights Stadium is not far," the super hero tells Alfred. "I'll start there."

Then the Dark Knight hits the gas, and the Batmobile speeds off.

Turn to page 62.

## *FWOOOOSH!*

Batman speeds through the night toward the Giordano Botanical Gardens. On the drive, he looks up the garden's map on the Batmobile's computer. Then he asks for "Orchid Display."

Just for safe measure, he also looks up "Boat Orchid" and learns there is a special display set up for these flowers.

Once at the gardens, the Batmobile screeches to a halt. Batman leaps out and heads to the orchid greenhouse. He is surprised that even at this late hour, the door is open.

The Dark Knight quietly creeps in, expecting there to be a trap.

Weaving his way through flower displays, he finds his way to the boat orchid display. A small open area with benches has been set up in front of it.

That's where he finds Tai, tied up.

Turn the page.

The Dark Knight breaks from his cover and goes over to help Tai. At his feet is a tangle of wires. Some connect to a black box directly under Tai's seat. Others wind their way around the bench to two potted flowers, one on each side of Tai on the bench.

*It could take hours to defuse this bomb,* Batman thinks.

He only has minutes left before it goes off.

Turn to page 58.

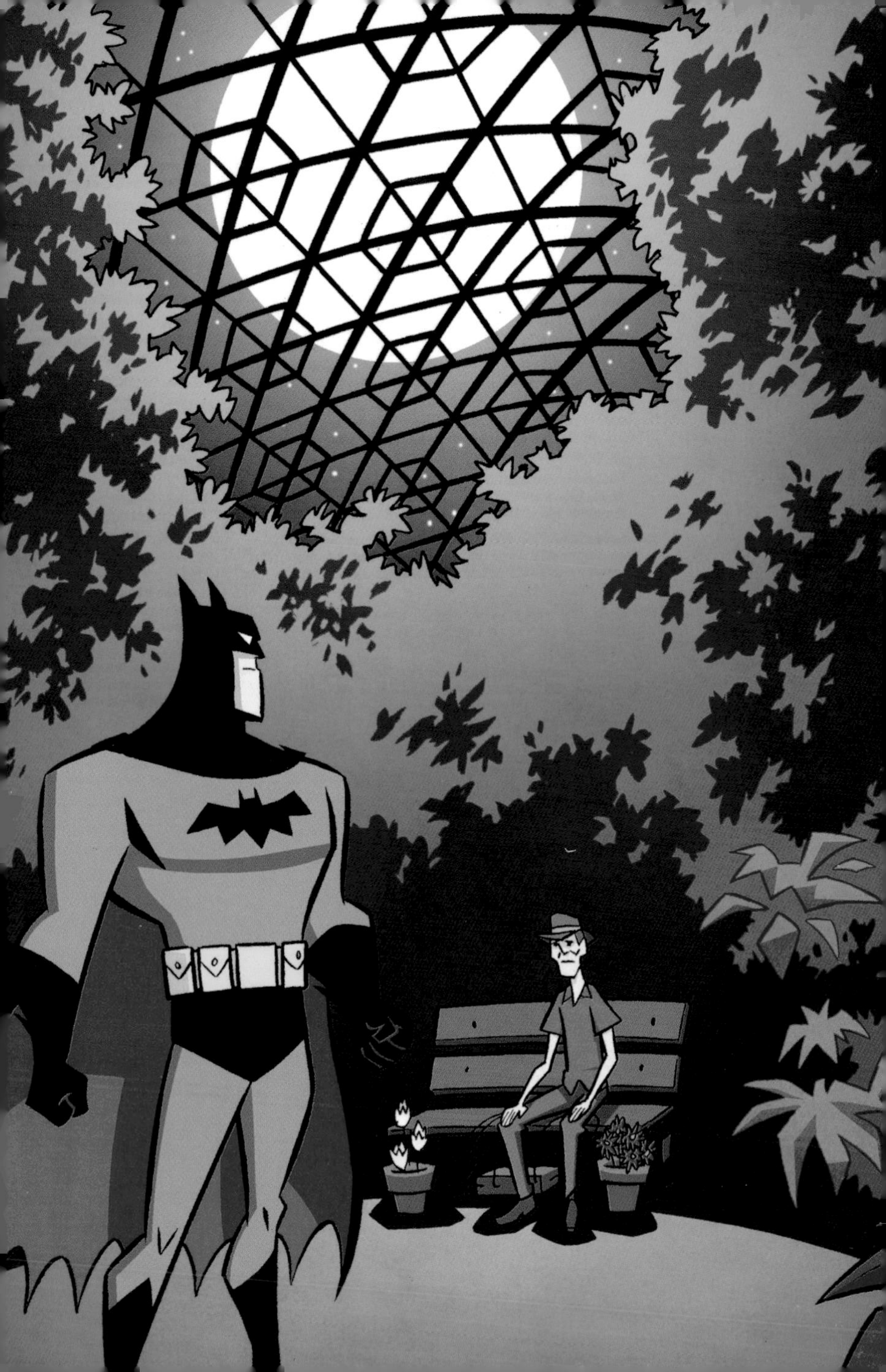

There is a note on Tai's lap. Batman picks it up and reads, WHICH FLOWER WILL GROW WHEN YOU PLANT KISSES?

Batman assumes he is to pick one of the potted flowers, which must answer the Riddler's riddle.

If Batman picks the tulips, turn to page 60.

If Batman picks the passionflowers, turn to page 63.

"Batman, are you there?" Alfred asks for the third time.

"Yes," the Dark Knight finally replies.

In front of him, he sees the fire blazing. The blare of sirens and flashing lights fill the night as emergency workers descend on the scene.

"Mr. Nakamura's near death has prompted your guests to raise the necessary money to free the rest of the Riddler's hostages."

*They must be scared that I will fail again,* Batman thinks.

Batman feels defeated, as if he failed to protect the city from a horrific crime.

Raising the money will at least prevent a tragic ending, but that means the Riddler gets away . . .

This time.

**THE END**

To follow another path, turn to page 7.

*Tulips, as in two lips, is the answer,* Batman thinks.

He reaches over and plucks the tulips from their pot.

Nothing.

Nothing happens, which means he guessed right.

Batman quickly unties Tai and then leads him out of the greenhouse.

"Alfred, I have rescued Tai," Batman says into his headset.

"By saving him," Alfred says, "your guests seem less willing to pay the Riddler's ransom."

"Then I'd better not fail in rescuing the other hostages," the Dark Knight responds.

"Steven Knight, owner of the Gotham Knights baseball team, was the second hostage taken," says Alfred.

As they talk, the Dark Knight rushes to the Batmobile.

Once inside, the super hero glances at the Gotham City map.

"The Knights Stadium is not far from here," Batman says. "I'll start there."

Turn the page.

Outside the Knights Stadium, near the main entrance, is a large video screen. During games, the screen displays the scores of games. It also lists special events, like concerts.

Tonight, an odd message flashes across the screen: IT GETS PRETTY BATTY IN HERE.

This clue is obviously meant for Batman's eyes. He parks the Batmobile and glances at the city map. He's not sure if it's a clue to enter the stadium or if it refers to another location. There are a couple places that the Riddler might be hinting at.

If Batman goes inside the Knights Stadium, turn to page 64.
If Batman heads to the belfry at the clock tower, turn to 68.
If Batman heads to Arkham Asylum, turn to 69.

*Kisses are passionate, so passionflowers are the answer,* Batman thinks.

He reaches over and picks the passionflowers from their pot.

There is a click.

Wrong guess!

The bundle of wires at Mr. Nakamura's feet begins to spark and smoke. The bomb must be faulty. Then suddenly, it bursts into flames!

Batman quickly grabs the bomb. He wraps the device in his fireproof cape, quickly extinguishing the flames. Then he rushes it safely outside.

While he waits for help disposing of the explosive, the Riddler is still on the loose, and this time he might just get away.

**THE END**

To follow another path, turn to page 7.

The stadium seems like the logical choice, and even more so, the batting cages. That's where Batman heads once he leaps over the locked entrance gate.

The night-vision lenses in his cowl allow him to sneak through the shadows. There's no sign of anyone. All is quiet, except for the chirps of crickets and the hum of vending machines. The place appears deserted.

"Alfred, he's not at the stadium," the Dark Knight says.

"You only have about fifteen minutes to find Mr. Knight," Alfred says. "No one here has raised any money to free him."

Just as Batman turns to leave, the stadium lights flick on. He stops. Feet stomp across turf. Half a dozen of the Riddler's henchmen, wielding baseball bats, surround him.

*A trap,* the Dark Knight thinks.

Then Batman leaps into action.

*FWOOSH!*

A henchman swings at his head. Batman ducks and delivers a kick to the gut, doubling his attacker over.

Then two more crooks approach. As they cock their bats back to ready their swings, Batman darts in, connecting his fists with their jaws.

During the melee, Batman notices that the stadium's scoreboard is ticking down the minutes.

Less than fourteen to go.

*I don't have time for this,* the super hero thinks.

Three henchmen are still standing as the other three slowly get to their feet. Batman takes a stun pellet from his Utility Belt and throws it to the ground.

*BANG!* A blinding light flashes. A deafening explosion roars. All of the attackers fall to the ground, covering their ears and eyes. Batman's cowl protects his eyes from the flash and dampens the sound of the explosion.

Turn the page.

The Dark Knight darts off and heads back to the Batmobile. He has precious little time to find the location of the next hostage.

He has two hunches where he might be located: the clock tower or Arkham Asylum.

If Batman heads to the belfry at the clock tower, turn to 67.

If Batman heads to Arkham Asylum, turn to page 69.

Maybe the Riddler meant "batty" like the phrase "bats in the belfry," meaning insane. Bats were often thought to roost in places high up, like clock towers.

But the clock tower is on the other side of town. Knowing the minutes are ticking down, Batman speeds through the night as fast as he can.

Turn to page 73.

"Batty" or "bats in the belfry" are similar terms, meaning insane. Batman's not sure why he made the connection, but he heads to the clock tower in southern Gotham City. It is a long way a way, so he speeds through the night as fast as he can drive.

Once at the clock tower, the Dark Knight creeps through a back entrance. The night-vision lenses in his cowl allow him to see as he darts up the steps that lead to the belfry.

Turn to page 73.

"Batty" is just another word for "insane," and Arkham Asylum is where the worst of Gotham City's mentally ill are kept. The Riddler even stayed there for a stint a few years back. That must be where the next hostage is located.

\*\*\*

Batman speeds off in the Batmobile. He radios ahead to the asylum's office, letting them know that he is coming.

The outside gates swing open for the Batmobile. A guard greets him at the entrance.

"Do you know which room Edward Nygma was locked in when he was here?" Batman asks.

"Edward who?"

"The Riddler," Batman says. Edward Nygma is his alter ego.

"This way."

Batman is shown to the Riddler's room. As they walk down the hallway, they see that the door is cracked open.

Turn the page.

"That's odd," the guard says.

He and Batman rush into the room. In the middle of it sits Steven Knight, tied to a chair.

In Steven's lap, Batman notices a folded-up note. He grabs it and reads:

A BOX WITHOUT A LID, YET IT HIDES A GOLDEN TREASURE.

Turn to page 72.

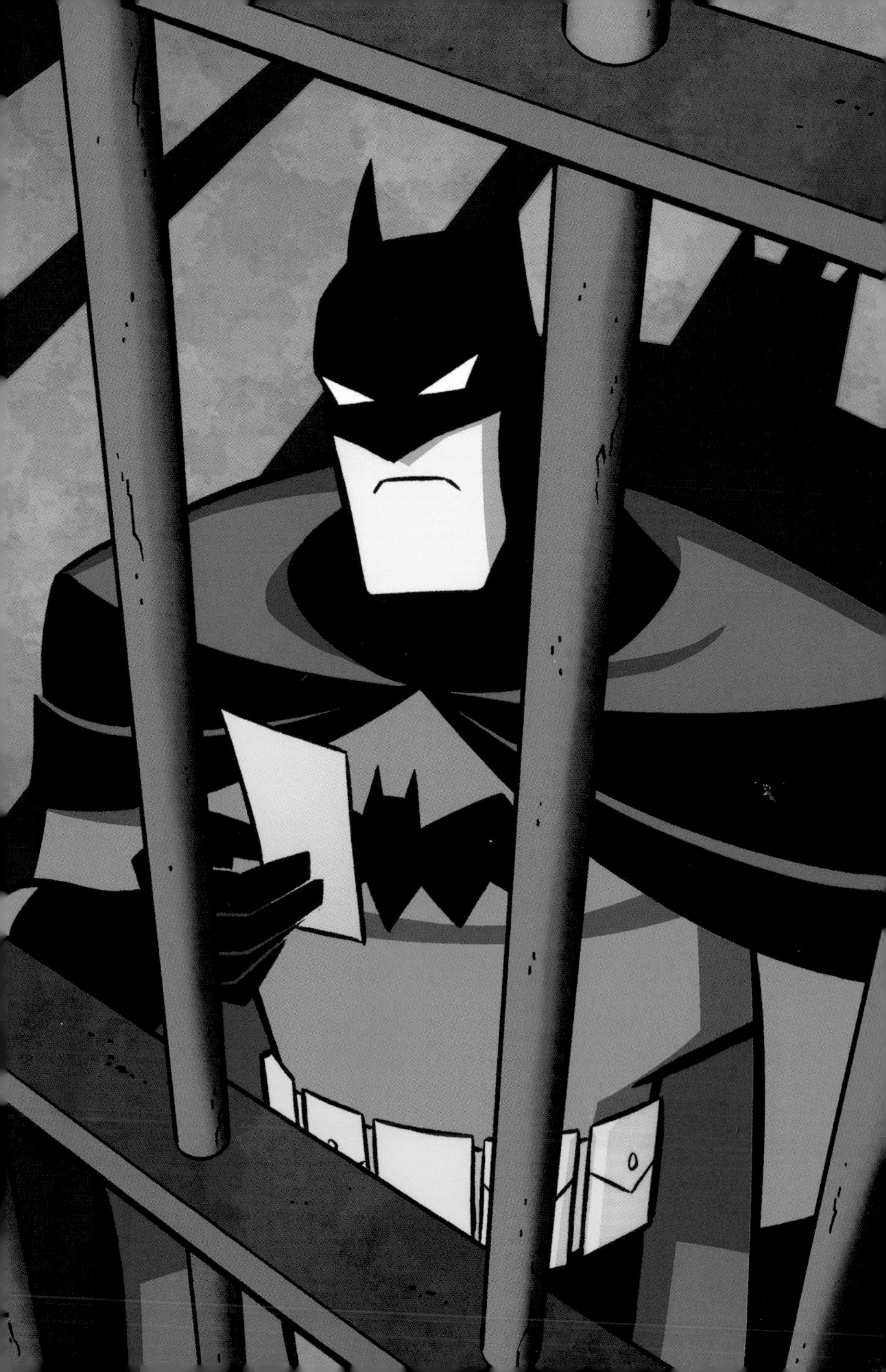

A web of wires lies at his feet. They connect a black box under Knight's seat to a small scale that sits in front of Steven. On one side of the scale is an egg. The other side, a coin purse.

Batman guesses he needs to take one of the items off the scale.

"How much time do we have, Alfred?" Batman speaks into his headset.

"Less than ten minutes," comes the reply.

It would be impossible to defuse this bomb in that amount of time, and Batman worries that moving Mr. Knight might set it off.

The Dark Knight must choose.

If Batman selects the egg, turn to page 75.
If Batman selects the purse, turn to page 77.

Once there, he creeps through a back entrance. The night-vision lenses in his cowl allow him to see as he rushes up the steps that lead to the belfry.

At the top of the tower, he is disappointed by what he finds.

Nothing.

Dust covers everything. No one has been up here in ages.

Just then, a brilliant explosion lights up the night. It comes from the direction of Arkham Asylum.

His guess was wrong, and a massive explosion destroys part of Arkham Asylum.

"Batman, are you there?" Alfred asks, concern in his voice.

"Yes," Batman finally replies.

The super hero sees the fire blazing. The blare of sirens screams across the distance, and flashing lights fill the night. Emergency workers descend on the scene.

Turn the page.

"The police just informed me that they have Mr. Knight," says Alfred. "He is safe, and your guests have raised the necessary money to free the rest of the Riddler's hostages."

*I still failed,* Batman thinks.

Even though the money will prevent a tragedy, Batman feels defeated. The Riddler got away with millions of dollars that could have helped the Martha Wayne Foundation.

**THE END**

To follow another path, turn to page 7.

*An egg has no lid, and the golden treasure would be its yellow yolk,* Batman thinks.

He picks up the egg. As he does, he sees Mr. Knight and the guard both wince, as if they weren't sure it was the right choice.

"I thought you should have picked the purse," the guard mutters.

"Me, too," Mr. Knight replies. A bead of sweat trickles down his forehead.

Batman notices that the scale doesn't move. It doesn't tilt toward the side holding the purse. Then he realizes that the egg in his hand hardly weighs anything at all.

He holds it up to the light above. Through the transparent shell, he sees a thin, rolled-up piece of paper.

*A clue!* he thinks.

Batman breaks the eggshell and then unrolls the sheet of paper:

WHAT HAS A MOUTH BUT CANNOT TALK? WHAT BRIDGE HAS ALREADY SPRUNG?

Turn the page.

*Hmm . . .* Batman thinks. He can guess a few answers for the first part of the riddle. But the second part stumps him.

"Alfred, who was the fourth hostage taken?" he asks, speaking into his cowl.

"Reynold Jardin, a European business owner," Alfred replies.

*That's no help,* Batman thinks.

But he does have two ideas. Both a river and a cave have a mouth but do not talk.

If Batman goes to the nearest cave, turn to page 78.
If Batman goes to the nearest river, turn to page 81.

*A purse has no lid, yet it can hold coins — even gold ones,* Batman thinks. So he picks the purse off the scale.

Once its weight has been lifted, the scale tilts, with the egg side dropping down.

### CLICK!

*The answer must have been the egg, with its golden yellow yolk,* Batman thinks as the bomb explodes.

### KA-BOOM!

Batman shields himself with his fireproof cape. The explosion rips the room apart. When the smoke clears, the Dark Knight is still standing, but he's covered in cuts and bruises. It'll be weeks before he's at full strength again.

In the meantime, the Riddler is free.

**THE END**

To follow another path, turn to page 7.

The Batcave is the closest cave. To get there, Batman needs to cross the Robert Kane Memorial Bridge, at the northeastern tip of Gotham City. He's not sure exactly how that bridge fits into the Riddler's riddle, but he's pretty confident the first part of the riddle refers to the caves north of the bridge.

Only a few people know the location of the Batcave. But it is part of a complex system of caves widely known for it large population of brown bats. Maybe somewhere between the caves and the bridge, Batman will find the Riddler's next hostage.

"Batman, where are you?" Alfred's voice speaks into Batman's headset.

"Just nearing the Robert Kane Memorial Bridge," Batman replies.

"Your guests here are getting nervous," Alfred explains. "You have less than fifteen minutes to rescue Mr. Jardin."

As he crosses the bridge, Batman is feeling the pressure.

He still has no idea as to exactly what the Riddler's last clue meant.

The minutes tick down.

Batman drives as close as he can to the location of the largest cave that people can actually get to. He hops out of the Batmobile and then scampers up to the cave's mouth.

With his night vision, the super hero peers into the cave. It's empty. There aren't even any bats, as they are out scouring the night sky for insects. He hopes they are having more success than he is with a certain criminal.

The Dark Knight turns to climb back down the hill. As he does, he sees a sudden flash off in the distance. An explosion near the Sprang Bridge lights up the night sky.

"Batman," Alfred's worried voice speaks into his headset. "What happened?"

Silence.

"Batman, are you there?" Alfred asks.

"Yes," Batman finally replies.

Turn the page.

The blare of sirens and flashing lights wake the sleeping city as emergency workers descend on the scene.

"Your guests have agreed to raise enough money to free the Riddler's remaining hostage."

That may be a relief to everyone involved, but not to Batman.

*I have failed,* Batman thinks.

He feels defeated. He may have saved a few lives tonight, but the Riddler got away with his crime — with a million dollars that could have helped the Martha Wayne Foundation.

**THE END**

To follow another path, turn to page 7.

The Sprang River flows around the island that Arkham Asylum sits on. Flowing east to west, the river separates the northern third of the city from the rest of Gotham City. There are also several bridges that cross its waters.

Then the answer hits Batman.

The first part of the clue is river. Then the answer to "what bridge has sprung" would be the Sprang Bridge.

The Riddler must be holding Mr. Jardin somewhere near the mouth of the Sprang River, where the Sprang Bridge is located.

Batman floors the gas pedal of the Batmobile. He has precious little time to get from the west side of Gotham City to its eastern shore.

At the northern end of the Sprang Bridge is a small park. Doing a quick survey of the area, the Dark Knight sees a green limo parked under a street lamp.

His guess was correct.

Turn the page.

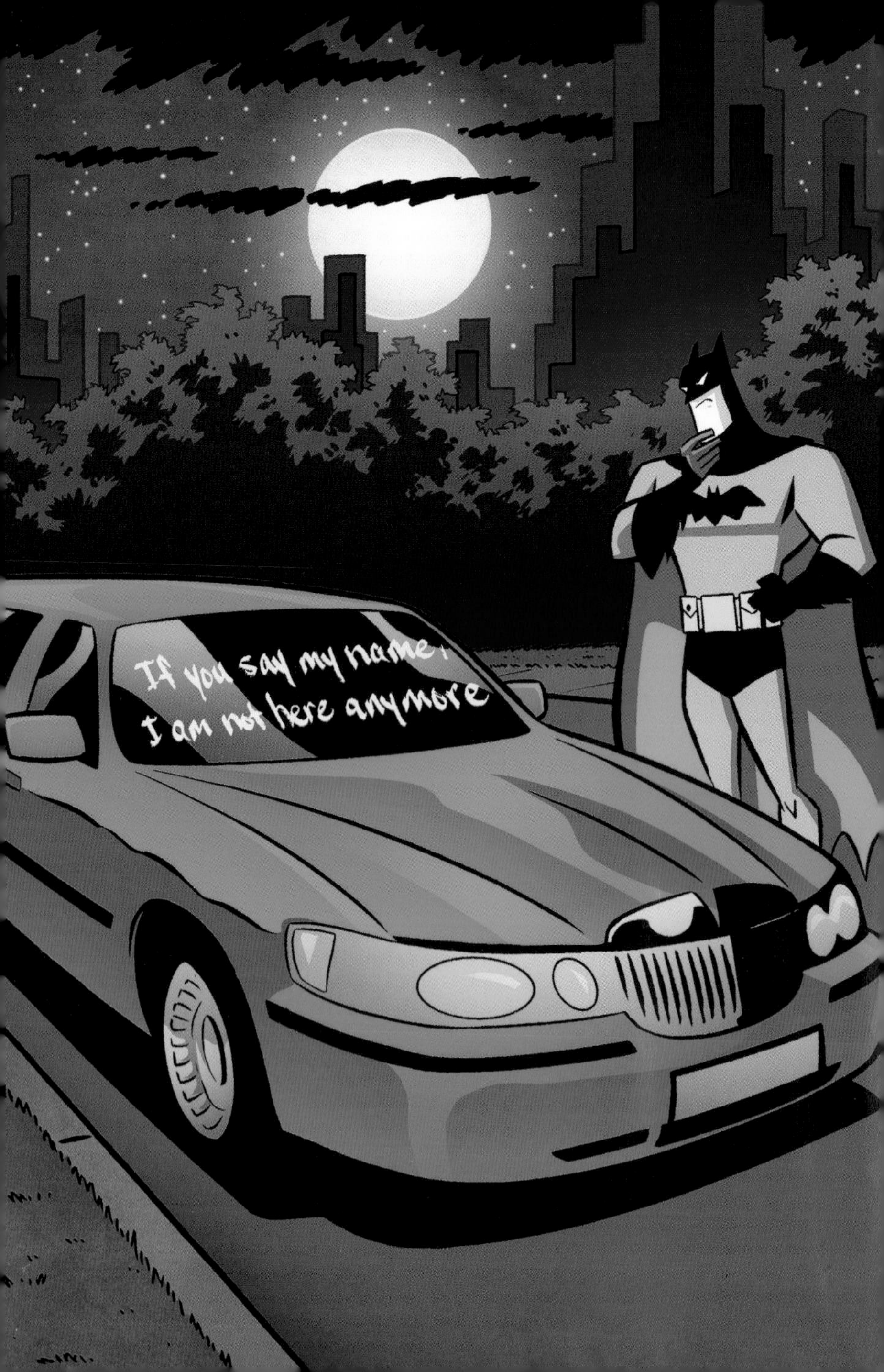
If you say my name,
I am not here anymore

Batman rolls the Batmobile to a stop about fifty feet from the limo.

As he walks over to it, the super hero notices some yellow writing scrawled across the car's windshield: "If you say my name, I am not here anymore."

*What could that mean?* Batman wonders.

Cautiously, he circles the car. He can't spot any noticeable traps, yet the Riddler wouldn't leave anything too obvious.

"Batman, have you found Mr. Jardin yet?" Alfred's voice speaks into Batman's headset. "Your guests here are getting nervous. I'm afraid they might attempt to leave."

Batman knows that if any of his guests leave before the Riddler's game is done that something terrible could happen.

If Batman replies that he has found Mr. Jardin, turn to page 87.

If Batman checks to make sure Mr. Jardin is in the car, turn to page 84.

Batman is confident that Mr. Jardin is in the green limo. He fears what might happen if he doesn't answer Alfred, telling him to prevent his guests from leaving before the Riddler's game is done. But just then he figures out the answer to the clue scrawled on the car's windshield.

*Silence. That is the answer. If you say it, say anything, then silence is gone.*

Batman flies into motion.

He fears that the slightest sound — an owl's hoot, a tugboat's toot, or the squeak of a shoe — might set off the Riddler's trap.

He opens the limo's back door slowly, so as not to make a sound. But it seems to have been well oiled to prevent any squeaks.

Inside the car, Mr. Jardin is tied up on the floor. Duct tape covers his mouth.

He turns to Batman and tries to mumble something through the tape, but Batman quiets him by placing a finger to his lips. He can't be too cautious in a moment like this.

As carefully and quietly as he can, Batman helps Mr. Jardin from the car.

Once safely away from the green limo, the Dark Knight pulls the tape from Mr. Jardin's mouth.

"Batman, I was told to tell you that my son is a big thief," Mr. Jardin says, spitting out the words.

"Is he, really?" Batman asks.

"No, I only have daughters," says Mr. Jardin. "But that's what those men in the green shirts told me to say."

"Alfred, I've rescued Mr. Jardin," the Dark Knight says.

"I will be sure to tell the rest of the guests," Alfred replies. "They are getting rather mutinous. You'd better find the last hostage quickly."

Batman thinks for a moment. His clue is that Mr. Jardin's son is a thief.

*Jardin*, he thinks.

Turn the page.

Once inside the Batmobile, he types that name into his computer. It translates to *garden* in Spanish, or possibly *park* in French.

Wayne Botanical Garden is the biggest garden in the city, while Robinson Park is the biggest park.

If Batman heads to Wayne Botanical Garden, turn to page 94.
If Batman goes to Robinson Park, turn to page 89.

Batman is confident that Mr. Jardin is the green limo. But he fears what might happen if any of his guests back at Wayne Tower leave the ballroom before the Riddler's game is done. He has already seen some of the bombs the Riddler has strapped to his hostages, and he's guessing that the final two hostages are in similar situations. The Riddler might just set those bombs off, killing two people — possibly more, if someone leaves the ballroom.

Batman feels he has to answer Alfred to prevent that situation.

He begins, "Alfred, I have —"

His words dispel the silence, and . . .

### KA-BOOM!

Before he can fully answer, an explosion rocks the limo. It bursts into a ball of flame as metal and plastic shrapnel whistle through the air.

"Sir, are you okay?" Alfred's trembling voice asks through the headset.

There is no answer.

Turn the page.

Then finally, the Dark Knight responds. "I'm okay, Alfred. Shaken but okay. I'm headed back to the Batcave. The Riddler has won . . . for now."

**THE END**

To follow another path, turn to page 7.

Suddenly the answer comes to Batman. A son that is a thief is a robbing son. Which could be shortened to Robinson, for Robinson Park.

The Dark Knight speeds off into the night. The Batmobile races through Gotham City.

Once at the park, Batman isn't sure what to look for. But the Riddler has made the hostages fairly easy to find, once he's found the correct location.

The minutes tick down.

Turn to page 91.

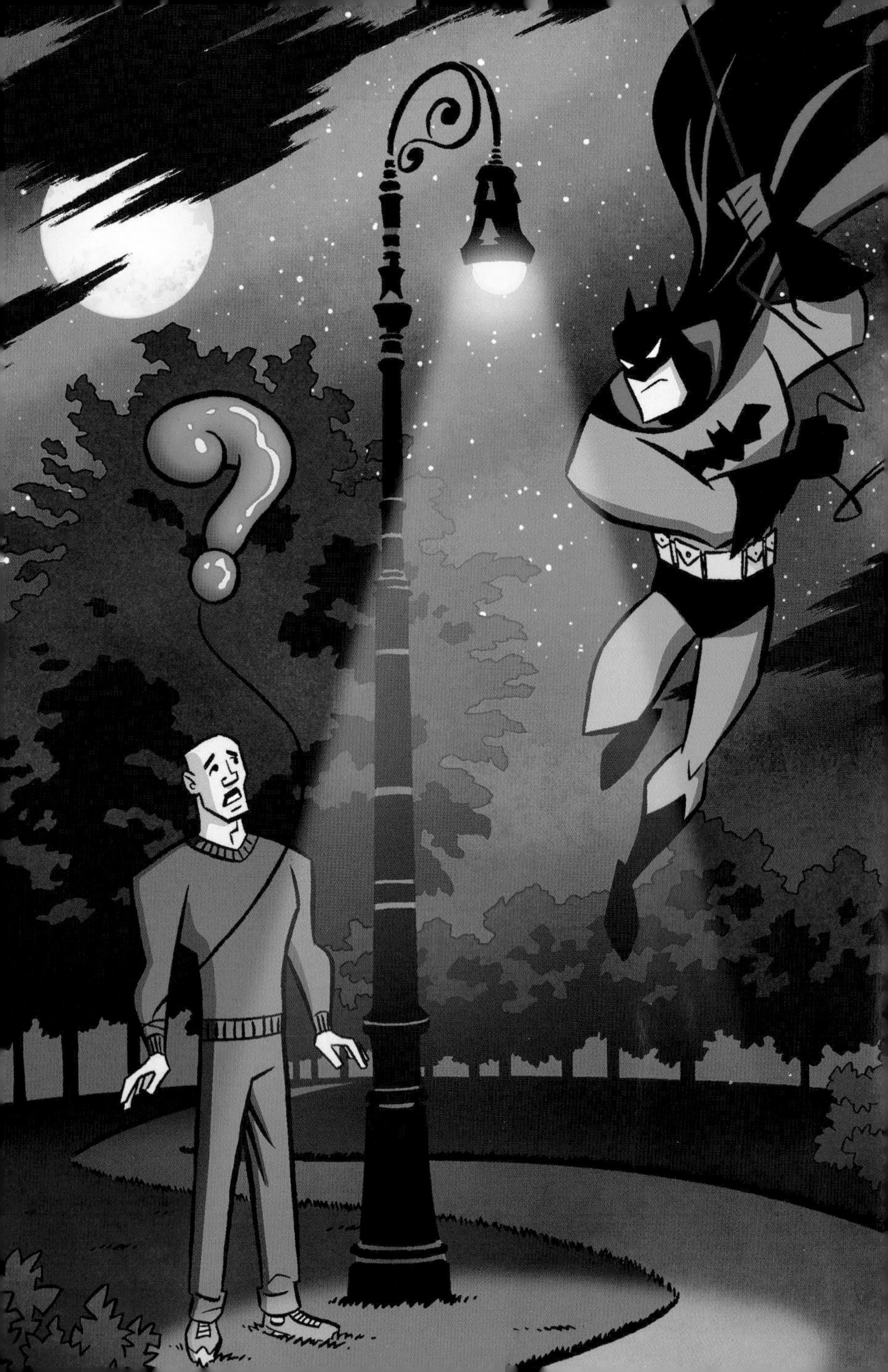

Toward the center of the park, Batman notices something odd: a giant green balloon shaped like a question mark. It is tied to a man who is standing all by himself in the middle of the park.

Batman rushes over to him.

"Are you okay?" he asks.

The man nods his head vigorously. "Yeah."

Batman circles him, looking for any signs of a bomb or a trip wire. He expects there to be some sort of booby trap, but nothing.

"Were you told to do or say anything?" Batman asks.

"No, just to stand still. Or there would be an explosion."

*Hmm,* Batman thinks. *It wouldn't surprise me if the Riddler had told the man that just to fool him.*

He tugs on the ropes binding the man.

"Hey, what are you doing?"

Turn the page.

Suddenly, there's a large **POP** as the balloon explodes.

From inside the balloon falls a note. Batman picks it up.

The note reads, WHAT HAS RIVERS WITH NO WATER, FORESTS WITH NO TREES, AND CITIES WITH NO BUILDINGS?

"Alfred, I have rescued the last of the hostages," he says into his headset.

"Can I tell your guests they are safe to leave?" Alfred asks.

"No, not yet," Batman replies. "There is one more riddle, so the Riddler's game isn't over yet."

Batman goes to the Batmobile. He is pretty sure what this last clue means, because he's been looking at the answer all night. On a monitor is a map of Gotham City.

He marks all the places that the hostages have been. They form a loose circle, and in the middle of that circle is Old Gotham, a dangerous part of town where criminals tend to hide out.

Perhaps he should include Wayne Tower, as the Riddler was also there tonight. But then things would look like a lollipop on the map.

If Batman considers the circle his next clue, turn to page 97.
If Batman considers the lollipop his next clue, turn to page 101.

## VROOOOM!

Batman speeds off to the Botanical Garden. He is not sure what all of the Riddler's riddle means — the part about Mr. Jardin's son being a thief. But he has come to the realization that the hostages the Riddler selected were not random. They are part of the clues that he's been following. So if Jardin translates into garden, he is going to check the city's biggest garden out.

\*\*\*

Moments later, Batman comes to a screeching stop outside the Wayne Botanical Garden. Since the garden has been named after his alter ego, Batman knows its layout well.

The Dark Knight exits the Batmobile and makes his way to the back door of the garden's main building. It's locked.

Batman knows the security code, but he decides not to use it. That action would alert others that Bruce Wayne had visited the garden. He cannot compromise his secret identity — even if that means making things a little difficult.

The Dark Knight reaches into his Utility Belt, which is filled with dozens of weapons and high-tech gadgets. He removes a small, rubberized pellet from one of the belt's compartments.

Batman squishes the pellet onto the keypad. The rubber glows red, and the Dark Knight quickly steps back. He shields himself with his fire-resistant cowl.

### KA-BLAM!

The pellet explodes, disabling the security keypad. The door to the garden swings open.

On the way over to the garden, Batman had been trying to think of what type of plant a thief might steal. That's when he had thought back to the boat, *The Orchid*, at Roger's Yacht Basin.

The Wayne Botanical Garden has some gold orchids in one of its greenhouses. The plants have an odd history, as an alchemist once thought they were key ingredients for turning ordinary rocks into gold. Gold was also part of a previous clue, the one about the egg.

Turn the page.

He is hopeful that he is on the right track.

When Batman reaches the gold orchids, he is surprised to find nothing. No one.

He pokes through the plants for clues that someone was there.

Nothing.

Then it hits him . . . *A son that is a thief is a robbing son,* he thinks. *Which could be shortened to Robinson.*

He is at the wrong location. It'll be too late for him to reach the other location in time. The Riddler has won for now.

**THE END**

To follow another path, turn to page 7.

Batman speeds off in the Batmobile. He uses the Batmobile's computer to find the location that is the exact center of the circle he had drawn using the locations of the hostages.

He drives up to a green building with a storefront that reads "Joke Shop."

*This could be it,* he thinks.

He parks the Batmobile out of sight. Then he goes around back to an alleyway and finds the back door locked. Using lock picks from his Utility Belt, he jimmies the door open.

Inside, it's quiet. And empty. Dust covers the floors. Cobwebs fill the corners.

He walks to the center of the shop. On the floor is a folded-up sheet of paper that seems too new to fit these surroundings.

He picks it up. A note inside reads, WHAT ASKS A QUESTION BUT NEVER ANSWERS.

*I can't believe I missed it!* The thought screams in his head.

He darts back to the Batmobile.

Turn the page.

Plopping down in the driver's seat, he looks at the map on his screen again. It's not a circle or a lollipop that he should have drawn, but a question mark. Using the locations of the hostages and Wayne Tower, the shape on the screen creates a rough question mark.

*And the point for that question mark is most likely Tricorner Yards,* he thinks.

Batman speeds to Tricorner Yards, a shipping dock along the southern shore of Gotham City.

He spends the rest of the night scouring the area for clues. Near sunrise, he finds a scrap of paper taped to a shipping container. It reads, WHAT NOUN FOOLED YOU WITH HIS LESS FUNNY CHILDREN?

*Hmm,* Batman thinks. *Funny is less funny than funnier, just like long is less long than longer. And it was the Riddler who fooled him, so . . .*

Then Batman cursed angrily.

*The Riddler,* he thinks. *The Riddler fooled him with riddles.*

While the Riddler may have gotten away tonight, Batman can at least take solace in the fact that he saved people's lives.

Maybe next time, he won't get fooled by the Riddler's riddles.

**THE END**

To follow another path, turn to page 7.

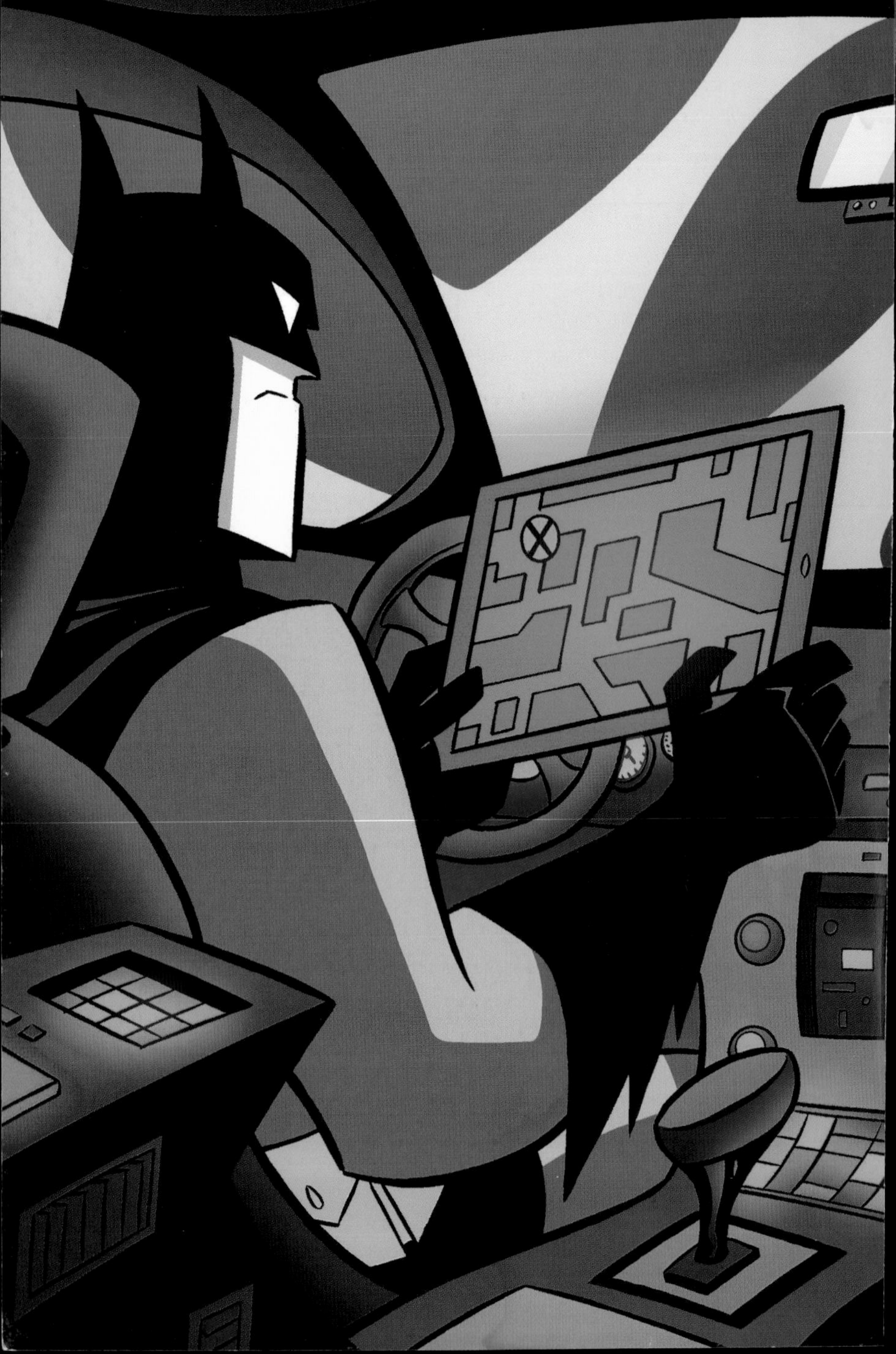

Staring at the map, an idea strikes him. The balloon in the shape of a question mark that had been tied to the man held a riddle with the answer of a map — the Riddler's symbol. Maybe it's not a lollipop that he should be drawing with all the locations. If he takes out the line between Arkham Asylum and Robinson Park, the locations form a question mark.

And . . .

The point of that question mark would be the Tricorner Yard, along the southernmost tip of Gotham City.

Batman hits the gas pedal and speeds off.

Turn the page.

Batman isn't sure how much time he has or if the Riddler knows that he has saved the last hostage. He doesn't know if the Riddler has been tipped off that he's on his way or, in his arrogance, if the Riddler figures that Batman would never be able to solve his riddles.

As he nears the yard, Batman turns off his headlights. He goes into night-vision mode. Once in the yard, he parks his car in the shadows and then searches the area on foot. The Riddler's location is easy to find. Outside a shipping container is parked a green limo. Four of the Riddler's henchmen are chatting as they pack up some computer equipment into the trunk.

"Hurry," one of them says. "The Riddler's mad that he didn't get any ransom money."

"Does that mean we don't get paid?" a second henchman asks.

"Which one of us is going to have to drive him back to headquarters?" a third asks nervously.

"Urk!" the fourth screams as Batman thunks him over the head.

As one of the henchmen charges, Batman sends a kick to his jaw, knocking the man to the ground.

The other two henchmen turn to flee. Batman takes two Batarangs from his Utility Belt. Each has a wire attached to it. He throws one, then the other, at the two men running away. The Batarangs swirl around the men, entangling them in the wires, and they fall to the ground.

Turn the page.

Then Batman goes to the limo. He crawls into the driver's seat — the glass divider is up, so the Riddler can't see who's up front.

Immediately a voice squeals at him over a speaker, "What has been taking you goons so long? We need to leave in case Batman figures out my last clue."

"We're heading out now," Batman says, trying to disguise his voice.

"Good, take me to my headquarters," the Riddler says.

"Sure thing, boss," Batman replies.

Batman revs the engine. Then he speeds out of the Tricorner Yards.

Gotham City Police Department Headquarters is not far away. He heads in its direction.

Batman pulls up to the front door of the police station. He gets out and rushes around to open the back door for the Riddler.

The Riddler steps out, looking up, confused, at the GCPD Headquarters sign.

"This isn't my headquarters . . ." he begins. Then he turns to see who opened the door for him. "Oh!"

Batman grabs the Riddler's arm and leads him inside to be booked.

**THE END**

To follow another path, turn to page 7.

# AUTHOR

Blake Hoena grew up in central Wisconsin, where he wrote stories about robots conquering the moon and trolls lumbering around the woods behind his parents' house. He now lives in St. Paul, Minnesota, with his wife, two kids, a dog, and a couple of cats. Blake continues to make up stories about things like space aliens and superheroes, and he has written more than seventy chapter books and graphic novels for children.

# ILLUSTRATOR

Ethen Beaver is a professional comic book artist from Modesto, California. His best-known works for DC Comics include Justice League Unlimited and Legion of Superheroes in the 31st Century. He has also illustrated for other top publishers, including Marvel, Dark Horse, and Abrams.

# GLOSSARY

**asylum** (uh-SYE-luhm)—a hospital for people who are mentally ill and cannot live independently

**cowl** (KOU-uhl)—a long hooded cloak

**elaborate** (i-LAB-ur-it)—complicated and detailed

**hostage** (HOSS-tij)—someone taken and held prisoner as a way of demanding money or other conditions

**investigate** (in-VESS-tuh-gate)—find out as much as possible about something

**philanthropist** (fuh-LAN-thruh-pist)—a person who helps others by giving time or money to causes or charities

**random** (RAN-duhm)—without any order or purpose

**ransom** (RAN-suhm)—money that is demanded before someone who is being held captive is set free

**unconscious** (uhn-KON-shuhss)—not awake and unable to see, feel, or think

# THE RIDDLER

Real Name:
**Edward Nygma**

Occupation:
**Professional Criminal**

Base:
**Gotham City**

Height:
**6 feet 1 inches**

Weight:
**183 pounds**

Eyes:
**Blue**

Hair:
**Black**

Even as a little boy, Edward Nygma loved riddles and puzzles. When he grew up, Nygma turned his passion into a career. He became a video game designer and soon invented a popular game called *Riddle of the Minotaur*. The game sold millions of copies, but Nygma didn't recieve a dime from the manufacturer. To get his revenge, Nygma became the Riddler, a cryptic criminal who leaves clues to his crimes.

- The Riddler carries a cane shaped like a question mark. This weapon can deliver a shocking blast – the Riddler's answer to his toughest problems.

- The Riddler doesn't just want to break the law. He wants to outsmart Batman as well. Before every crime, the Riddler first sends a clue to Batman.

- The Riddler's real name suits him perfectly. Edward Nygma, or E. Nygma for short, sounds like the word "enigma," which means a mysterious person.

- Harry Houdini is one of the Riddler's greatest heroes. This real-life magician is famous for his stunts, tricks, and great escapes.

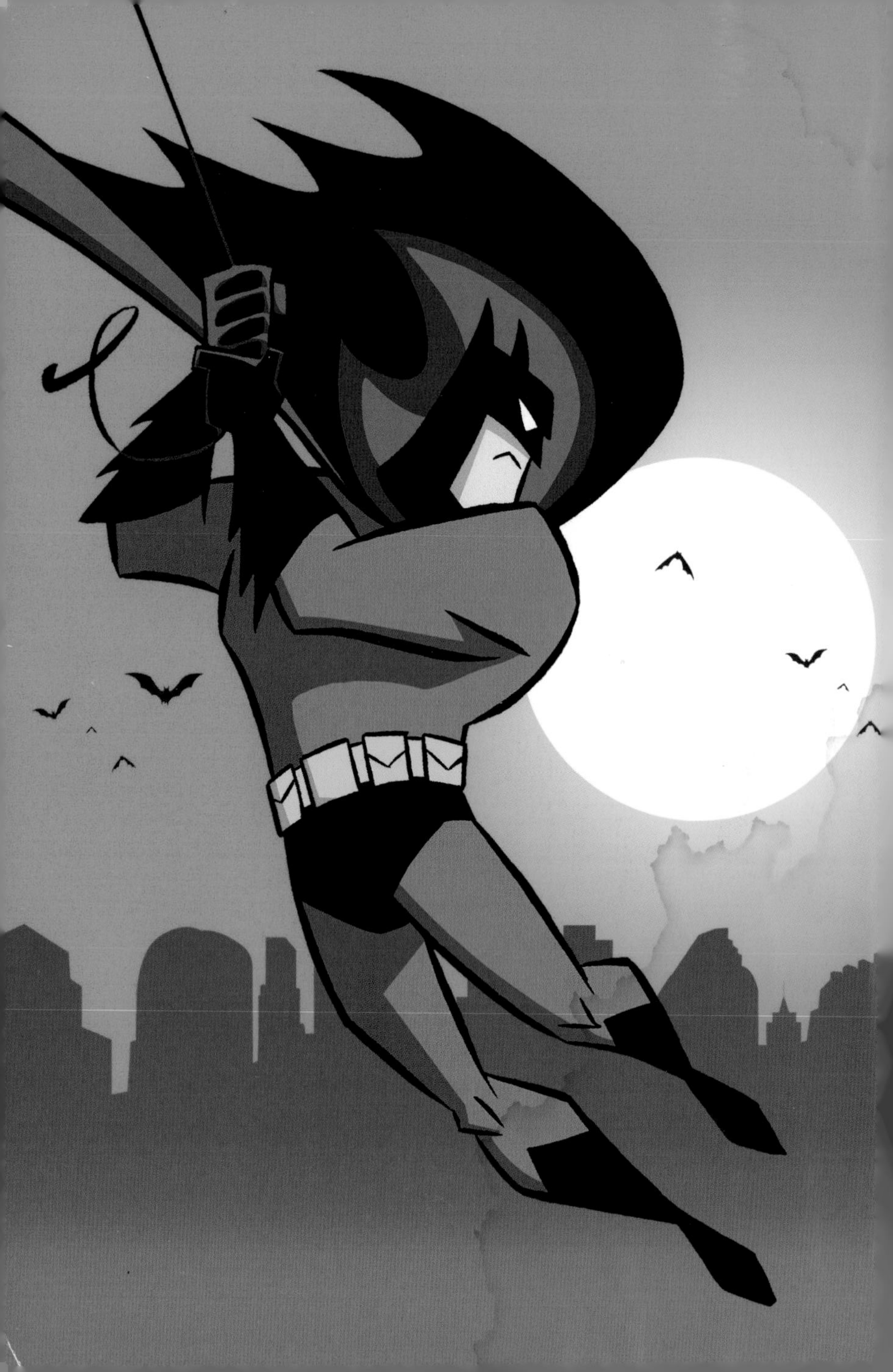

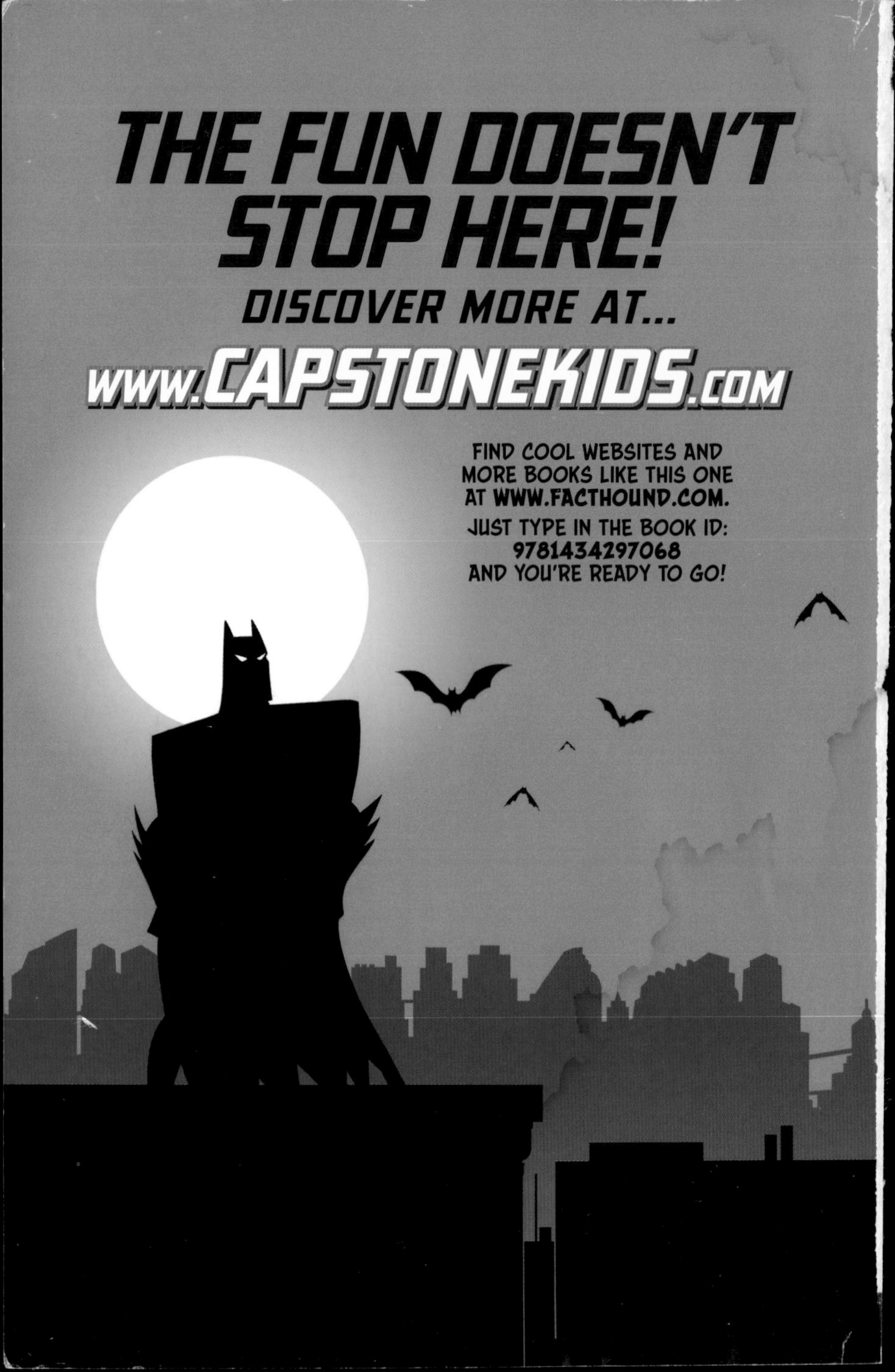
THE FUN DOESN'T STOP HERE!
DISCOVER MORE AT...
WWW.CAPSTONEKIDS.COM
FIND COOL WEBSITES AND MORE BOOKS LIKE THIS ONE AT WWW.FACTHOUND.COM.
JUST TYPE IN THE BOOK ID: 9781434297068 AND YOU'RE READY TO GO!